John L. Shorey

The Beautiful Book for Little Children

John L. Shorey

The Beautiful Book for Little Children

ISBN/EAN: 9783337416935

Printed in Europe, USA, Canada, Australia, Japan

Cover: Foto ©Andreas Hilbeck / pixelio.de

More available books at **www.hansebooks.com**

THE

BEAUTIFUL BOOK

FOR

LITTLE CHILDREN.

BOSTON:
JOHN L. SHOREY.
1875.

GIFT OF

.

BOSTON:
RAND, AVERY, & CO., STEREOTYPERS AND PRINTERS.

CONTENTS.

CONTENTS.

THE BEAUTIFUL BOOK.

"A THING of beauty is a joy forever," says the poet; and so we cannot too soon begin to teach the child to recognize and love the beautiful.

We here give him the beautiful in art, and the beautiful in thought; and, if he has not yet learned to read, the parent or teacher will here find the means of teaching him with ease and speed.

The method is plain and natural, like that of teaching a child to speak. Point to the words of a line in their order, and see that he gives his attention to their form, size, and sound. Repeat this patiently, and for a short time every day; and you will soon be surprised at his progress.

Do not trouble yourself, as yet, about the alphabet, or the analysis of syllables; and let the little pupil himself choose the piece that you are to drill him on.

It is true that memory, in fixing the words in his mind, may often lead him to glance too inattentively at their *forms.* But memory will prove more a help than a bar, even here; for it will serve the place of a teacher, by telling him what the words are when he *does* attend, and thus enabling him to study them out by himself.

A great advantage of the word-system is, that, to the child himself, it makes learning to read a pleasure instead of a toil.

The numerous pictures are, it is believed, of a character to develop and improve a taste for art.

This volume, with " The Easy Book," which is in prose, will not only serve as a quick and easy means of teaching a child to read, but will help to inspire in him a genuine love of letters; and thus it is, in fact, not only a beautiful, but a practically useful book.

All the contents are from " The Nursery," a magazine for youngest readers, issued monthly by the publisher of this volume.

Autumn Leaves

THE leaves, they are falling, falling, falling:
  Red, brown, and yellow, I see them fall.
The birds, they are calling, calling, calling:
  Swallows old and young, I hear them call.
Come, Mary! Come, Jamie! Come, Harry and Kate!
See the leaves and the swallows: come, do not be late.

7

The warm days, they are going, going, going:
　　Come, mount the hill with me before they go.
The little brooks are flowing, flowing, flowing;
　　But very soon they all will cease to flow.
For the leaves are falling, falling; the swallows flying, flying;
And soon the winds of winter will be sighing, sighing, sighing.

The autumn bees are humming, humming, humming:
　　Soon they will be silent all and still.
Said the children, "We are coming, coming, coming:
　　Wait there for us, Uncle Charley, on the hill.
Come summer, come winter, come heat, or come snow,
We're bound to be merry wherever we go."

THE ACORNS.

"TALL oaks from little acorns grow."
　　Yes, darling children, that is so:
　　Then plant your acorns; do not fear;
　　And fruit will by and by appear.
　　The line you learn to-day may be
　　The very seed of Wisdom's tree.

LIFE'S MORNING AND EVENING.

"GRANDMOTHER, tell me, were you young once, and little, like me ?
 Golden and brown was your hair ? smooth and unwrinkled your skin ?
 Could you once frolic and run round in the garden, like me ?
 Grandmother, had you a doll ? Did you love flowers and birds ?
 Shall I a grandmother be ? totter along with a cane ?
 Might one not stay ever young on this bright, beautiful earth ? "

MARCH.

MARCH is a funny old blustering fellow:
He whistles his tunes from morning till night;
He scatters the ground with crocuses yellow,
    Then frosts them over with white.

Up in the morning, 'mid sunshine playing,
And then, in an hour, drifting the snow;
Then stopping, he thinks of the children's Maying,
    And silently ceases to blow.

With smiling and sighing, and raining and snowing,
He tries to catch up with the mild April showers,
And help them to moisten the valleys for sowing,
    And wake up the exquisite flowers.

Moody and fitful, his footsteps are ranging
From morrow to morrow, till April is near;
Then kissing her face, with its tremulous changing,
    He leaves there a smile and a tear.

Then mute with the sight of her wonderful graces,
While shadows of night veil his sobbing retreat,
In a tumult of rain the last snow he effaces,
    And meltingly dies at her feet.

MABEL AND THE SNOW-DROPS.

In April, when snow-drops were
  blooming,
  Our dear little Mabel was born;
And as sweet to the eye as a snow-
  drop
  Has she been ever since, every
  morn.

She minds every word that we tell
  her;
  She loves to give food to the poor;
She treats all dumb creatures with
  kindness,
  And they all love her dearly, I'm
  sure.

I hope that all children who hear me
  Will shun, like our Mabel, all vice;
Will keep pure and bright as the
  snow-drop,
  That blooms amid snow-drifts and
  ice.

THE JOHNNY-CAKE

This is the seed,
So yellow and round,
That little John Horner hid in the ground.

These are the leaves,
So graceful and tall,
That grew from the seed so yellow and
small.

This is the stalk,
That came up between
The leaves so pretty and graceful and
green.

These are the tassels,
So flowery, that crowned
The stalk, so smooth, so strong, and so
round.

These are the husks,
With satin inlaid,
That grew 'neath the tassels that drooped
    and swayed.

This is the silk,
In shining threads spun:
A treasure it hides from the frost and the
    sun.

This is the treasure, —
Corn yellow as gold, —
That satin and silk so softly unfold.

This is the cake,
For Johnny to eat,
Made from the corn so yellow and sweet.

A COLD DAY.

JACK FROST is a roguish little fellow:
When the wintry winds begin to bellow,
He flies like a bird through the air,
And steals through the cracks everywhere.

He nips little children on the nose;
He pinches little children on the toes;
He pulls little children by the ears,
And draws from their eyes the big round tears.

He makes little girls cry, "Oh, oh, oh!"
He makes little boys say, "Boo — hoo — hoo!"

But when we kindle up a good warm fire,
Then Jack Frost is compelled to retire;
So up the chimney skips the roguish little boy,
And all the little children jump for joy!

MY CLOTHES-PINS.

My clothes-pins are but kitchen-folk,
    Unpainted, wooden, small;
And for six days in every week
    Are of no use at all.

But when a breezy Monday comes,
    And all my clothes are out,
And want with every idle wind
    To go and roam about,

Oh! if I had no clothes-pins then,
    What would become of me,
When roving towels, mounting shirts,
    I everywhere should see!

"I mean," a flapping sheet begins,
"To rise and soar away."
"We mean," the clothes-pins answer back,
"You on this line shall stay."

"Oh, let me!" pleads a handkerchief,
"Across the garden fly."
"Not while I've power to keep you here,"
A clothes-pin makes reply.

So, fearlessly I hear the wind
Across the clothes-yard pass,
And shed the apple-blossoms down
Upon the flowering grass.

The clothes may dance upon the line,
And flutter to and fro:
My faithful clothes-pins hold them fast,
And will not let them go.

My clothes-pins are but kitchen-folk,
Unpainted, wooden, small;
And for six days in every week
Are of no use at all.

But still, in every listening ear,
Their praises I will tell;
For all that they profess to do
They do, and do it well.

LEARNING TO WALK.

Who comes here?
  Little boy John,
Brave as a lion:
  See him come on!

What does he want?
  A kiss, I am thinking:
Come, sir, and take it;
  Come without winking!

Don't be afraid
  Of a stumble or fall;
For Johnny must walk,
  Although he is small.

First one little foot,
  Now forward the other:
That's right! here you are,
  My own little brother!

GRANDFATHER'S CHAIR.

I LOVE, when the evenings are balmy and still,
And summer is smiling on valley and hill,
To see in the garden the little ones there,
All happy and smiling round grandfather's chair.

Such stories he tells them,—such tales of delight,—
Such wonders to dream of by day and by night,
It's little they're thinking of sorrow and care,
Their bright faces beaming round grandfather's
    chair.

And words, too, of wisdom, fall oft from his
    tongue ;
Dear lessons to cherish and treasure while young ;
Bright things to remember when white is their
    hair,
And some of them sit in a grandfather's chair.

Ah ! little ones, love him, be kind while you may,
For swiftly the moments are speeding away ;
Not long the kind looks and the love you may
    share,
That beam on you now from a grandfather's chair.

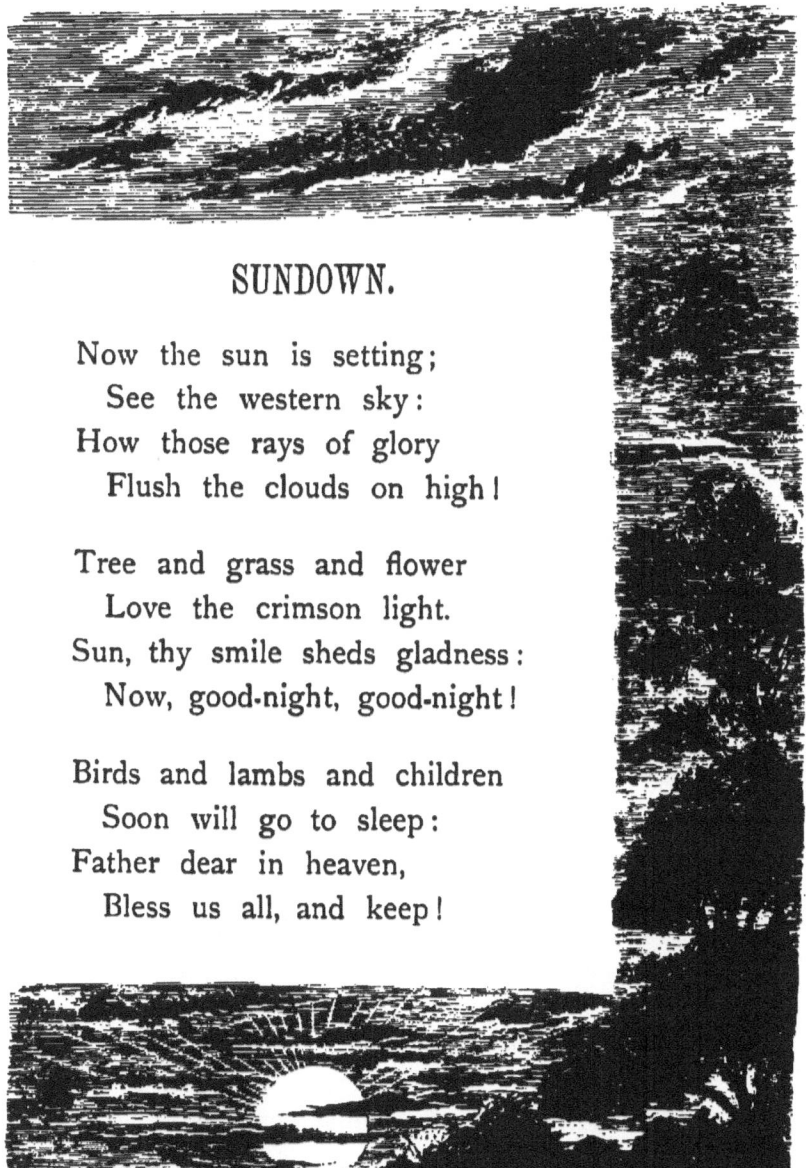

SUNDOWN.

Now the sun is setting;
  See the western sky:
How those rays of glory
  Flush the clouds on high!

Tree and grass and flower
  Love the crimson light.
Sun, thy smile sheds gladness:
  Now, good-night, good-night!

Birds and lambs and children
  Soon will go to sleep:
Father dear in heaven,
  Bless us all, and keep!

TIZ–A–RING.

" Tiz-a-ring, tiz-a-ring !
What a funny song to sing !
You're a cunning little thing,
   Busy bee, busy bee !
Though you fly so far and long,
And your wings are good and strong,
Yet you sing no other song,
   Busy bee, busy bee !

" I am sure, if I were you,
I would learn a tune or two
From the birds that sip the dew
   By your side, busy bee !
So that with your gauzy wing
You might fly, and sweetly sing
Something else but tiz-a-ring,
   All the day, busy bee ! "

" I'm too busy, don't you see,
To be learning melody,"
Quoth the cunning little bee,
   And went hurrying along.
" Tiz-a-ring may sound but queer
To my little critic's ear ;
But you'll like my honey, dear,
   If you do not like my song."

A LITTLE TEASE.

I KNOW a little fellow
  Who is such a wilful tease,
That, when he's not in mischief,
  He is never at his ease:
He dearly loves to frolic,
  And to play untimely jokes
Upon his little sister,
  And upon the older folks.

He rings the bell for Sarah,
  And then slyly runs away;
And tries to make a fool of her
  A dozen times a day:
He hides away in corners,
  To spring suddenly in sight;
And laughs, oh! very heartily,
  To see her jump with fright.

When kitty's lying quiet,
  And curled up warm and snug,
This little fellow always feels
  Like giving her a hug;
And kitty from his fond embrace
  Would surely never flinch,
Did she not know the little tease
  Would give her many a pinch.

But this provoking fellow
  Has a very curious way
Of feeling rather hurt at tricks
  That other people play, —
Just like some older jokers,
  Who laugh at fun they make,
But never can enjoy the fun
  Of jokes they have to take.

CAROL FOR SPRING.

WINTER is done!
Daisies are lifting their heads to the sun;
Mayflowers, smiling the soft winds to greet,
Burst into loveliness sudden and sweet;
Primroses, pale as with looking on snow,
Crocuses, violets, see how they grow!
Robins and bluebirds make nests in the sun:
Winter is done!
Sister of Summer, your reign is begun!

Winter is done!
Out of its death all this glory is won!
Down at the roots where the fallen leaves cling,
Wrecks of the Autumn make blossoms for Spring;
Dust of the rose-leaves gives bloom to the rose;
Life out of death thus eternally grows;
Earth's blooming children come back one by one:
Winter is done!
Sister of Summer, your reign is begun!

MAY.

Sunny day, joyful day,
Do not go so fast away ;
For this is the month of May,
And we love to have you stay.

On the banks, in sunny nooks,
In the meadows, by the brooks,
Better even than story-books,
Wild flowers charm us with their looks.

See ! you need not wander far :
Birds are singing, " Here they are !"
Sunny day, joyful day,
Do not go so fast away !

TOMMY'S ADVICE TO THE CROW.

CROW, crow, you look very grave :
But people *do* whisper that you are a knave ;
That you lurk in the fields to pilfer our corn ;
And a robber have been from the time you were born.

Crow, crow, you wear a black coat ;
And you never indulge in a blithe, jolly note :
But for all your gravity, sir, I think
You are worse than the madcap bobolink.

He does not dress nor talk like a saint ; .
He drawls not, nor preaches ; he uses no paint:
But he lets our corn and our rye alone ;
And he carries away no food but his own.

A little honesty, sir, would be
The better for you and the better for me :
Stop being a robber, stop breaking the law,
Or doff your black habit, and never say, " Caw."

24

PAPA. AND THE DOLL.

OH the pretty lady Doldy!
With her fresh, round, rosy face,
With her rich, red Garibaldi,
Trimmed around with tatted lace:
See her watch too; real Geneva!
Well, now, that's the time o' day.
I'm ashamed of my old lever:
It was never half so gay.

How her golden hair is shining!
Who has curls so fair and bright?
Just like sunny tendrils twining
Round her eyes, blue beads of light:
What an arm! how nicely rounded!
What a soft and dimpled hand!
How the taper wrist is rounded
With the bracelet's jewelled band!

Hold her up, my little Mary ;
Let me see the titmouse feet,
Small enough for any fairy,
With morocco shoes so neat :
Pray don't let her walk a distance,
Or you'll never keep them bright.
What, not walk without assistance !
Oh, dear me ! perhaps you're right.

Ah ! I'm sure she's smiling at me
With her dainty coral lips :
Does she want to come and pat me
With those tiny finger-tips ?
No, my dear, I will not take her.
I am not a tender nurse ;
I might rumple, squeeze, or shake her ;
Let her fall ; that would be worse.

Well, your nursery's quite a model,
Fitted up so smart and gay :
Round it little Ned can toddle,
You and Sister Rosa play.
Doldy's cradle, too, for certain :
Do just let me have a peep !
Oh ! how sweet behind that curtain
Blue-eyed beauty soon will sleep !

I'll not stay while you undress her,
And put on her bed-gown white :
I will stoop and gently kiss her ;
Whisper in her ear, "Good-night."
You must wake her in the morning,
All her things in order placed ;
In her robing and adorning
. Show the very nicest taste.

THE LITTLE VOLUNTEERS.

THREE cheers! three cheers
For the little volunteers!
Oh, what a merry sight it is to see them pass,
Knee-deep in buttercups and ankle-deep in grass!
Tramp, tramp, tramp, as onward they go
Over the old fence to rush upon the foe.
One with a rake, and another with a cane, —
Now look out for the wounded and the slain!
Three cheers! three cheers
For the valiant volunteers!

27

The curly-headed captain is not very large:
See him scale the fence, and lead the fearful charge!
The corporal who follows sees the captain fall,
Just as he jumps down into the clover tall;
Then, what with Nero's barking and the cackling
 of the geese,
I have to tell the army they must keep the peace.
   But three cheers! three cheers
   For the little volunteers!

THE SNOW-DROP.

DARLING little snow-drop,
 Coming up so boldly,
While the winds of winter
 Yet are blowing coldly!
When the ponds were freezing,
 Blooming I have found you,
Little milk-white flower,
 With the snow all round you!

Do you come so early,
 In these wintry hours,
Just to tell us kindly,
 Spring is near with flowers?
Darling little snow-drop,
 Hope and joy you lend us:
God still loves his children, —
 Loves, and will befriend us!

ON THE WAY TO SCHOOL.

Susan, Henry, John, and Joe,
See them there all in a row:
On their way to school they go.

They have learned their lessons well;
They can read, and they can spell;
They of lakes and towns can tell.

They start early on their way,
And stop not to climb and play,
Though it is a pleasant day.

But, when school at last is done,
They'll be ready all for fun:
They will frolic, climb, and run.

SEE ALL THE SWALLOWS.

COME back to us, dear swallows!
For Spring your coming follows:
    To your old nest beneath our eaves,
      come back!
We love to see you dearly,
You feed your young so queerly,
  · And bring sweet hopes of summer in
      your track.

DEAR LITTLE MARY.

DEAR little Mary,
  Susan and Loo,
Jenny and Lizzie,
  And Margaret too;
Now the sun's peeping,
  Softly and sly,
In at the window,
  Pets, where you lie!

Up, up, my darlings,
  Up and away!
Out to the meadows
  Sweet with new hay;

Out where the berries,
  Dewy and red,
Hang in great clusters,
  High overhead!

Out where the golden-rod
  Bends on its stalk,
And the wild roses
  Gladden our walk;
Where amid bushes
  Hidden but heard,
Joyous and grateful
  Sings many a bird.

Out where the waters,
  Merry and sweet,
Ripple and tinkle
  Close by your feet;
Where all things happy,
  Fragrant, and fair,
In the bright morning
  Welcome you there!

THOUGHTLESS little Peter, with his little gun,
Went out by the woodside for a little fun :
Saw a happy little hare who on clover fed ;
With his little gun took aim, and shot him in the head.

Thoughtful little Peter, sad for what he'd done,
Sat down on a stump, and there, by it, laid his gun ;
Wished that he could bring to life that little hare so still :
"Never more," said he, " will I a harmless creature kill."

THE CAT-BIRD.

"Sweet, sweet! tyr-ril, tyr-ril, tyr-ree!"
The cat-bird on the cherry-tree, —
How gayly and how loud he sings,
As on the blooming bough he swings ! —
"Tyr-ril, tyr-ree!" His mate he calls,
His carol with the blossoms falls.

Oh ! when he's pleased, search far and wide,
No sweeter singer's known ;
But then, alas ! the cat-bird has
A temper of his own.

And if, by chance, his will is crossed,
At once his spite he shows, —
"Maow, maow! pay, pay!" his song is changed ;
And all the music goes.

If he can have, to build his nest,
The place that pleases him the best ;
If winds are soft, and skies are bright,
And all the world with him goes right, —
"Tyr-ril, tyr-ree!" you never heard
A sweeter-voiced, more charming bird.

But if his mate to him should say,
"I mean, for once, to have *my* way;"
Or if a sparrow, or a thrush,
The withered grass should take,
That he had thought to use himself,
When he his nest should make ;

Or if, too near his chosen tree,
His head a robin shows, —
" *Maow, maow! pay, pay!* " his song is changed ;
And all the music goes.

O cat-bird! 'mid the falling flowers
Upon the cherry-tree,
How many people I have seen,
That were, how much like thee !

From cheerful homes and loving hearts,
Too well, alas! I know,
There's nothing like a temper-fit
To make the music go.

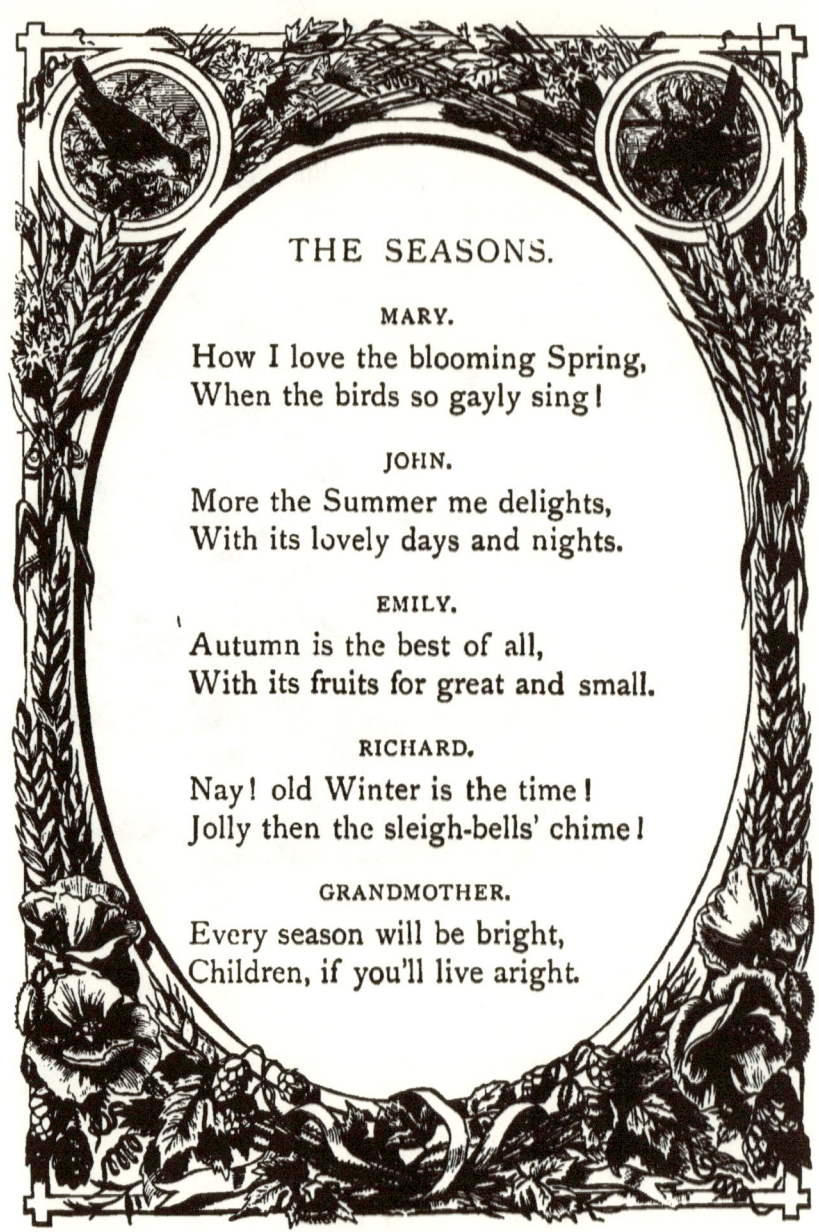

THE SEASONS.

MARY.

How I love the blooming Spring,
When the birds so gayly sing!

JOHN.

More the Summer me delights,
With its lovely days and nights.

EMILY.

Autumn is the best of all,
With its fruits for great and small.

RICHARD.

Nay! old Winter is the time!
Jolly then the sleigh-bells' chime!

GRANDMOTHER.

Every season will be bright,
Children, if you'll live aright.

POP-CORN! WHO'LL BUY?

Who will buy my pop-corn? —
Bags of snowy pop-corn,
  Freshly done to-day.
When they're fairly popping,
You should see them hopping,
  Like a school at play.
      Pop-corn! Who'll buy?

Who will buy my pop-corn? —
Pretty balls of pop-corn,
  Sweet, and creamy white;
Just like snowballs blowing,
In the garden growing,
  Good for taste or sight.
      Pop-corn! Who'll buy?

THE BABY IN THE BASKET.

" Now, where are you going, this beautiful day?"
" Good sir, I am going to help rake the hay."
" But you must be weary and worn, I'm afraid.
    With that heavy load on your back, little maid."
" Oh, no, sir! the load is not heavy to me:
    The load is my own baby-sister, you see."
" I see; and this lesson I get from the sight:
    Love makes labor easy and any load light."

LITTLE DILLY-DALLY.

I DON'T believe you ever
  Knew any one as silly
As the girl I'm going to tell about,
  A little girl named Dilly.
    Dilly-dally-Dilly!
      Oh! she is very slow:
    She drags her feet
    Along the street,
      And dilly-dallies so!

She's always late for breakfast,
  Without a bit of reason;
For Bridget rings and rings the bell,
  And wakes her up in season.
    Dilly-dally-Dilly!
      How can you be so slow?
    Why don't you try
    To be more spry,
      And not dilly-dally so?

'Tis just the same at evening;
  And it's really quite distressing
To see the time that Dilly wastes
  In dressing and undressing.
    Dilly-dally-Dilly
      Is always in a huff
    If you hurry her,
    Or worry her,
      And says, "There's time enough."

Since she's neither sick nor helpless,
  It is quite a serious matter,
That she should be so lazy, that
  We still keep scolding at her.
    Dilly-dally-Dilly,
      It's very wrong, you know,
    To do no work
    That you can shirk,
      And dilly-dally so.

BABY'S WALK

On a bright and a beautiful summer's day,
Mr. Baby thought best to go walking away :
His little white sack he was well buttoned in :
And his shady hat was tied under his chin.

One hand was tight clasped in his nurse's own ;
The other held fast a little white stone :
There hung by his side his new tin sword ;
And thus he began his walks abroad.

He walked and he walked ; and by and by
He came to the pen where the piggy-wigs lie :
They rustled about in the straw in front ;
And every piggy said, " Grunt, grunt, grunt ! "

So he walked and he walked ; and, what do you think !
He came to the trough where the horse was at drink :
He cried, " Go along !   Get up, old Spot ! "
And the horse ran away with a trot, trot, trot.

So he walked and he walked ; and he came at last
To the yard where the sheep were folded fast :
He cried through the crack of the fence, " Hurrah ! "
And all the old sheep said, " Baa, baa, baa ! "

So he walked and he walked till he came to the pond,
Of which all the ducks and the ducklings are fond :
He saw them swim forward, and saw them swim back ;
And all the ducks said was, " Quack, quack, quack ! "

So he walked and he walked ; and it came to pass,
That he reached the field where the cows eat grass ;
He said with a bow, " Pray, how do you do ? "
And the cows all answered, " Moo, moo, moo ! "

So he walked and he walked to the harvest-ground ;
And there a dozen of turkeys he found :
They were picking the grasshoppers out of the stubble ;
And all the turkeys said, " Gobble, gobble, gobble ! '

So he walked and he walked to the snug little house
Where Towser was sleeping as still as a mouse :
Then the baby cried out, " Halloo, old Tow ! "
And the dog waked up with a " Bow, wow, wow ! "

So he walked and he walked, till he came once more
To the sunshiny porch and the open door ;
And mamma looked out with a smile, and said,
" It's time for my baby to go to bed."

So he drank his milk, and he ate his bread ;
And he walked and he walked to his little bed ;
And with sword at his side, and the stone in his hand,
He walked and he walked to the Sleepy Land.

MY LINNET.

WOFUL bereavement! O hap-
   piness fled!
O grief for to-day and to-morrow!
   My linnet, my bright, merry linnet,
      is dead:
Come, birdlings, come join in my
      sorrow.

Then came all the dear little birds to the call, —
   The thrush and the finch and the sparrow,
The blackbird, the robin, the woodpecker, all,
   The swallow, too, swift as an arrow.

Four took up the bier, and the rest fluttered on
   To the grove where the woodbine was twining;
For all of them loved the dear bird that was gone;
   And even the flowers seemed repining.

Above the green turf where their burden was laid,
   They chirped their regret as they hovered:
The robin a heap of the sweetest leaves made,
   And with it the lifeless form covered.

THE NURSERY ELF.

Dear little feet, how you wander and wander,
    Little twin truants, so fleet!
Dear little head, how you ponder and ponder
    Over the things that you meet!

Dear little tongue, how you chatter and chatter
    Over your innocent joys!
Oh! but the house is alive with your clatter, —
    Shaking, indeed, with your noise.

Can't you be quiet a moment, sweet rover?
    Is there no end to your fun?
Soon the "old sand-man" will sprinkle you over,
    Then the day's frolic is done.

Come to my arms, for the daylight is dying,
    Closer the dark shadows creep;
Come like a bird that is weary of flying;
    Come, let me sing you to sleep.

ITS VERY BEST.

THE snow-flakes fall like thistle-down;
The wind blows cold without:
There's not one thing that seems like spring
But this potato-sprout!
And this is but a sorry sight,
It looks so weak and thin and white.
"Oh, yes!" says the potato-sprout,
"I've never had the light;
Yet, poorly as I look, I know
I've tried my very best to grow.

"When dropped the red and yellow leaves,
The farm-boy threw me in
The very darkest corner of
The darkest cellar-bin.
I did not see one sunny ray ;
I could not tell the night from day:
But, when long weeks had worn away,
I felt it must be spring, and so
I tried my very best to grow.

"Could I be planted in the ground,
And feel the sun and showers,
I should rise tall and straight and green,
And have a crown of flowers.
Oh! judge me not by what you see:
I am not what I want to be!
The sun has never shone for me;
But in the dark, at least, I know,
I've tried my very best to grow."

44

FLOWER–TALK.

WHAT does the crocus say?
"Summer sunshine's on the way."

What does the wind-flower sing?
"We are the footprints of spring."

What says the columbine?
"April showers make me fine."

What does the violet speak?
"Those who want me, they must seek."

Breathes the lilac's rich perfume,
"Children love my purple bloom."

What has the king-cup told?
"All the fields I fringe with gold."

"Sweetness," whispers mignonette,
"Follows where my feet are set."

What does the pansy sigh?
"Balm for wounded hearts am I."

Nods the sunflower in her bed,
"See the glory round my head!"

Sweet-brier blushes, "Who would hold
What he prizes, must be bold."

THE RUDE PLAYMATE.

"Oak-leaf and maple-leaf!" Hear the wind call:
"Beech-leaf and willow-leaf, flutter and fall!
Red leaves and yellow leaves, orange and brown,
Dance on the shaken boughs, dance, and come down!
I'll be your playfellow; careless and gay,
We will keep sporting through all of the day:
Up in the air, or about on the ground,
Merrily, merrily whirling around,
Hither and thither, wherever I blow,
Over the hills and the fields you shall go.

"Red leaves and yellow leaves, flutter and fall!
Come to me, come to me!" Hear the wind call.
Fair are his promises. Off from the bough,
Down comes a pretty red maple-leaf now.
Poor little thing! By to-night it will be
Wishing again it were back on the tree.
Rude is the wild wind, and rough is his play;
Hardest of labor is sporting all day.

SPRING RAIN.

WHILE it patters, while it pours,
Little folks are kept indoors;
Little birds sing through the rain,
" Dreaming flowers, awake again !
From the damp mould lift your bloom;
Make the earth sweet with perfume."

And the flowers, one and all,
Answer to this cheery call:
Crocuses begin to thrill;
Violets thicken on the hill;
And the fields and meadows over,
Shines the white and crimson clover,

When it patters, when it pours,
Little folks are kept indoors,
Looking through the window-pane,
Watching the unceasing rain ;
While its silver voice repeats,
" Blossoms crown the earth with sweets."

THE BEAR AND THE BEE-HIVE.

" HERE's a feast ! " said the sly old bear ;
" Pots of honey, I do declare !
Scold as you will, you noisy bees :
I'm big enough to do as I please."

Then the little bees came out in a swarm,
And Bruin began to be very warm ;
And, though the old fellow was pretty tough,
He soon felt ready to cry, " Enough ! "

WHO IS TO BLAME?

"Now, what can this mean?
  Who is having a ride
At this time of night,
  With his eyes open wide?
I left Johnny snug
  In his own little bed:
Now see him high up
  By somebody's head!

"Come! whom shall I punish?
  Now, who is to blame?"
Cried Johnny, "Papa,
  Papa, is his name.
He found me awake,
  And watching a star:
So do not scold *me*,
  But scold *him*, mamma!"

THE REAPERS.

EVERY morn,
Among the corn,
The reapers are busy and blithe;
And a song they sing,
As they merrily swing
Around them the glittering scythe.

They see the lark,
Like a tiny spark,
Far up in the blue, blue sky;
And beneath their feet
The dewdrops sweet
Like millions of diamonds lie.

SLEEPING IN THE SUNSHINE.

SLEEPING in the sunshine,
    Fie, fie, fie!
While the birds are soaring
    High, high, high!
While the buds are opening sweet,
And the blossoms at your feet
Look a smiling face to greet.
    Fie, fie, fie!

Sleeping in the sunshine,
    Fie, fie, fie!
While the bee goes humming
    By, by, by!
Is there no small task for you,—
Nought for little hands to do?
Shame to sleep the morning through!
    Fie, fie, fie!

GOING FOR VIOLETS.

THREE little maidens,
    Pretty and good,
Seeking for violets,
    Went through the wood.
They saw a bluebird;
    They saw a sparrow;
They met a small boy
    With bow and arrow.

" Don't shoot the birdies!"
    Cried they all three:
" Come and hunt violets
    By the pine-tree."
" I'll break my arrow,"
    Said the small boy;
" And in the violets
    I'll find my joy."

THE TARDY BOY.

A DIALOGUE.

MOTHER.	ROBERT.
SEE! the hour for school is near:	Mother, mother, do not fret!
Robert, Robert, do you hear?	I'm not through my breakfast yet.

MOTHER.

From your bed you should have sprung
When the early bell was rung.

ROBERT.

All my window-panes were white
With the frost we had last night.

MOTHER.

If you would not be a dunce,
Brave the cold, and rise at once.

ROBERT.

When Jack Frost is in the case,
Bed is such a pleasant place !

MOTHER.

He who loves his bed too well
Never, never, will excel.

ROBERT.

Mother, mother, do not scold :
I shall soon be eight years old.

MOTHER.

More's the shame for you, my son,
Leaving duties thus undone !

ROBERT.

Something whispers in my ear,
You are right, my mother dear.

MOTHER.

Then get down sir, from your stool,
And run quickly off to school.

ROBERT.

Off I go ! You shall not see
After this a drone in me !

ONLY A BABY SMALL.

ONLY a baby small,
   Dropt from the skies ;
Only a laughing face,
   Two sunny eyes ;
Only two cherry lips,
   One chubby nose ;
Only two little hands,
   Ten little toes ;
Only a golden head,
   Curly and soft ;

Only a tongue that wags
   Loudly and oft ;
Only a little brain,
   Unvexed by thought ;
Only a little heart,
   Troubled with nought ;
Only a tender flower,
   Sent us to rear ;
Only a life to love
   While we are here.

MARY'S SLEIGH-RIDE.

OVER the meadow, and over the snow,
  Slippetty, slippetty, slip,
See Mary travelling while the winds blow,
  Nippetty, nippetty, nip !

What careth she for the ice and the cold ?
  Poppetty, poppetty, pop !
Pushed on so fleetly by Tommy the bold,
  Hoppetty, hoppetty, hop !

Carlo is barking at sight of the fun,
  Puppetty, puppetty, pup !
Home to the tea-table see Billy run,
  Suppetty, suppetty, sup !

WHEN SANTA CLAUS COMES

A GOOD time is coming: I wish it were here ! —
The very best time in the whole of the year:
I'm counting each day, on my fingers and thumbs,
The weeks that must pass before Santa Claus comes.

Good-by for a while, then, to lessons and school ;
We can laugh, talk, and sing, without "breaking the rule ;"
No troublesome spelling, nor writing, nor sums :
There's nothing but play-time when Santa Claus comes.

I suppose I shall have a new dolly, of course, —
My last one was killed by a fall from her horse ;
And for Harry and Jack there'll be trumpets and drums,
To deafen us all with, when Santa Claus comes.

I'll hang up my stocking to hold what he brings ;
I hope he will fill it with lots of nice things :
He *must* know how dearly I love sugar-plums ;
I'd like a big box full when Santa Claus comes.

Then when the first snow-flakes begin to come down,
And the wind whistles sharp, and the branches are brown,
I'll not mind the cold, though my fingers it numbs ;
For it brings the time nearer when Santa Claus comes.

IN THE MORNING.

THE sun is up; and its cheerful rays
  Shine, all things round adorning.
A sluggard is he in bed who stays:
  Like the sun, let us rise in the morning.

The silv'ry brooklet goes purling past,
  All bright in the early dawning;
It seems to run onward twice as fast:
  Like the brook, let us run in the morning.

The thrifty wild bees are flying out,
  All sloth and slumber scorning;
O'er field and garden they're humming about:
  Like the bee, let us work in the morning.

CHERRY BLOSSOM

LITTLE Cherry Blossom
  Lived up in a tree,
And a very happy
  Little thing was she.

Clad all through the winter
  In a dress of brown,
Warm she was, though living
  In a northern town.

But one sunny morning,
  Thinking it was May,
"I'll not wear," said Blossom,
  "This old dress to-day."

Mr. Breeze, this hearing,
  Very kindly said,
"*Do* be careful, Blossom:
  Winter has not fled."

Blossom would not listen;
  For the sky was bright,
And she wished to glisten
  In her robe of white.

So she let the brown one
  Drop and blow away,

Leaving her the white one,
  All so fine and gay!

By and by the sunshine
  Faded from her view:
How poor Blossom shivered
  As it colder grew!

Oh for that warm wrapper
  Lying on the ground!
Ah! Jack Frost will nip her:
  He is prowling round.

Yes, he folds poor Blossom
  In his arms of ice,
And her white robe crumples,—
  Robe so fine and nice!

Ah! poor Cherry Blossom!
  She, in foolish pride,
Changed her wonted clothing,
  Took a cold, and died.

All ye little blossoms,
  Hear me, and take care:
Go not clad too thinly,
  And of pride beware.

MAMMA'S BOY.

" BABY, climbing on my knee,
Come and talk a while to me.
We have trotted up and down,
Playing horse, all over town.
Whose sweet darling are you, dear?
Whisper close to mamma's ear:
Tell me quickly, for you can."
" I'm mamma's boy, but papa's man!"

" Why, you've many miles to go
Ere you'll be a man, you know.
You are mamma's own delight;
You are mamma's diamond bright;
Rose and lily, pearl and star,
Love and dove, — all these you are."
" No!" the little tongue began:
" I'm mamma's boy, but papa's man!"

THE SLEEPY BOY.

I KNOW a little boy;
And I've often heard it said,
That he never was so tired
That he wished to go to bed.
Though he scarcely can hold up
His drowsy little head,
Yet this very foolish boy
Cannot bear to go to bed.

When the big golden sun
Has lain down to sleep;
When the lambs every one
Are lying by the sheep;
When underneath its wing
Every chick tucks its head, —
Still this odd little boy
Does not like to go to bed.

Primroses and daisies
Have shut their bright eyes;
Grasshoppers and crickets
Are singing lullabies;

The fire-flies have lighted
Their lamps bright and yellow;
And I'm sure it's dreaming-time
For this sleepy little fellow.

The houseless little child
Who has no place to sleep;
Who on the ground must lie,
Or in some doorway creep;
O'er whom no clean white sheet,
No blanket soft, is spread, —
How happy he would be
If he could " go to bed "!

But with a pretty nest
All warm and soft and white,
That's waiting for this boy,
When it's time to say " Good-night ؛ "
With mamma's loving kiss,
And her hand upon his head, —
How strange a sleepy boy
Should not like to go to bed !

TOMMY AND THE WOODCHUCK.

A PRETTY brown woodchuck once made a snug hole
In a garden belonging to good Farmer Cole,
Where every thing grew that was pleasant to eat,
From big-headed cabbage, to jolly red beet.

There bloomed the gay flowers you all love so well, —
The many-hued aster, the bonny blue bell,
Pinks, daisies, and tulips ; while sun-flowers tall,
Like yellow-haired sentinels, guarded the wall.

At the door of his house, on a carpet of green,
The woodchuck oft sat, and surveyed the fair scene :
" This is truly a very fine garden !" quoth he,
" And doubtless 'twas planted on purpose for me."

So he nibbled, and ate, and he rolled in the clover,
As blithe as a lark, and as plump as a plover ;
Or he slept in his hole, far from tumult and noise,
Not worried by dogs, nor molested by boys.

Farmer Cole (worthy man !) saw him day after day ;
But he never attempted to harm nor to slay :
For said he, " Since we've plenty, and God gave it all,
We may well spare enough for a creature so small."

Our hero at last took a fancy to roam
Far away from the quiet seclusion of home ;
And while on his travels, — oh, grievous to tell ! —
A very unpleasant adventure befell.

Having climbed o'er the wall, through a field he must pass,
Where buttercups sprinkled the tall waving grass ;
While, hidden and lost in a cool, shady nook,
Danced o'er the white pebbles a rollicking brook.

'Twas a pleasant enclosure, and under the trees
The farmer's cow Brindle was grazing at ease ;
Her tail as she ate, like a long-handled mop,
Going flipperty-flopperty, flipperty-flop.

Now, little Tom Bowers, a mischievous elf,
Who chanced to be fishing there all by himself,
As bad luck would have it, the woodchuck espied,
And, seizing the rifle which lay at his side,

Shouted, " Now for some fun ; for, as sure's I'm a sinner,
I'll have that fine fellow served up for my dinner ! "
But, when you're too certain, take heed lest you fail :
Poor Tom missed his aim, and shot off the cow's tail !

The woodchuck sped home, nor behind him once glanced !
With anger and pain Brindle capered and danced ;
Then, plunging at Tommy, her horns fiercely shook,
And tossed him, head foremost, right into the brook !

Tom scrambled out quickly, both sadder and wiser;
Old Brindle's tail grew in a way to surprise her ;
And the woodchuck, content with his snug little hole,
Never more left the garden of good Farmer Cole.

KIND MAMMA.

THIS is not the old woman who lived in a shoe :
She has seven children, and knows what to do ;
She gives them some honey on nice home-made bread ;
She reads them a story, then puts them to bed.

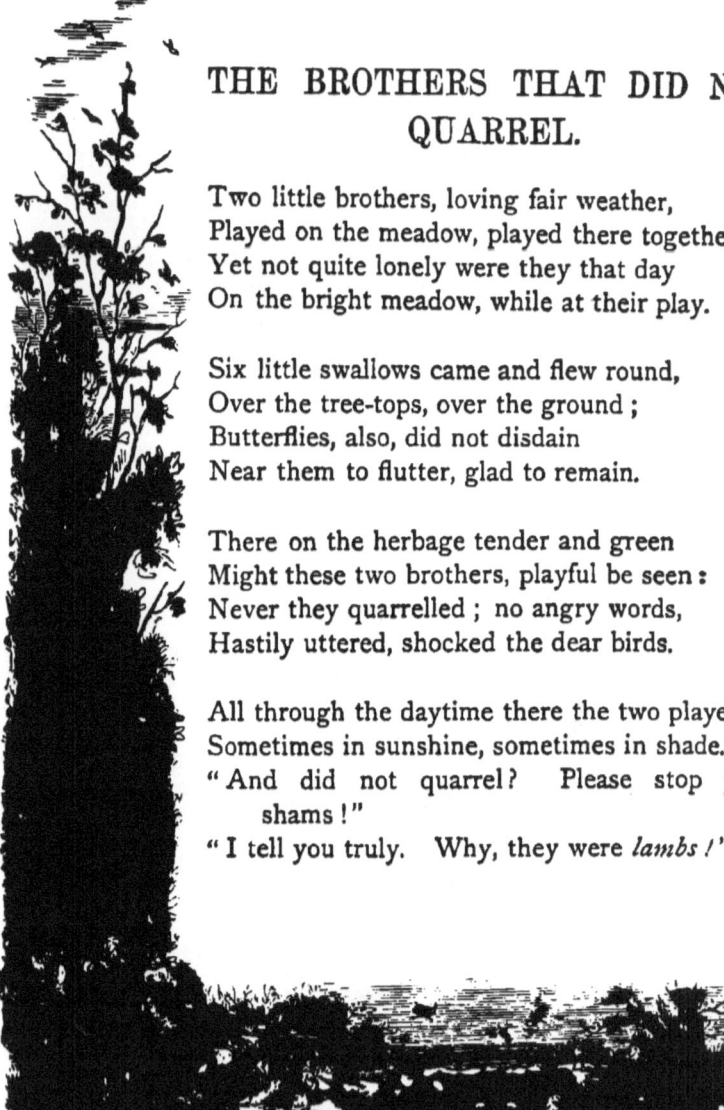

THE BROTHERS THAT DID NOT QUARREL.

Two little brothers, loving fair weather,
Played on the meadow, played there together ;
Yet not quite lonely were they that day
On the bright meadow, while at their play.

Six little swallows came and flew round,
Over the tree-tops, over the ground ;
Butterflies, also, did not disdain
Near them to flutter, glad to remain.

There on the herbage tender and green
Might these two brothers, playful be seen :
Never they quarrelled ; no angry words,
Hastily uttered, shocked the dear birds.

All through the daytime there the two played,
Sometimes in sunshine, sometimes in shade.
" And did not quarrel?   Please stop your
        shams !"
" I tell you truly.   Why, they were *lambs !* "

SUNRISE.

COME and see the sunrise,
  Children, come and see ;
Wake from slumber early,
  Wake, and come with me.
Where the high rock towers,
  We will take our stand,
And behold the sunshine
  Kindling all the land.

You shall hear the birdies
  Sing their morning lay ;
You shall feel the freshness
  Of the new-born day ;
You shall see the flowers
  Opening to the beams,
Flooding all the tree-tops,
  Flashing on the streams.

SUMMER.

SUMMER is in the air, odors are everywhere;
  Idle birds are singing loud and clear;
Brooks are bubbling over; heads of crimson clover
  On the edges of the field appear.

All the meadow blazes with buttercups and daisies,
  And the very hedges are tangles of perfume;
Butterflies go brushing, all their plumage crushing,
  In among this wilderness of bloom.

The thorn-flower bursts its sheath, the bramble hangs a wreath,
  And blue-eyed grasses beckon to the sun;
While gypsy pimpernel waits, eager to foretell
  When rainy clouds are gathering one by one.

The very world is blushing, is carolling and gushing
  Its heart out in a melody of song;   [ing,
While simple weeds seem saying, in grateful transport pray-
  " Unto Him our praises all belong !"

THE FANCY-DANCE.

SHALL I play you a waltz, or a jig ?
A hornpipe, a march, a cotillon ?
Take your choice; for I don't care a fig:
I'll scrape you out tunes by the million.

Choose partners ! All right ! To your places !
Come, Ponto, and make your best bow :
Take your steps; show the ladies what grace is.
A bow, sir, is not a bow-*wow*.

Off you go ! round and round, hand in hand !
Right and left ! Promenade down the middle !
Keep it up now ! Oh ! isn't it grand
To know how to play on the fiddle !

THE SONG OF THE DUCKS.

SPRING is coming, spring is here!
All ye ducks and geese, draw near!
Come and join us in our folly;
All ye waddlers, come, be jolly!
   Quack, quack! — quack, quack, quack!
Good soft mud and running water
   Now we shall not lack, — not lack!

See, the snows are melting, going,
And the little streams are flowing;
Buds are swelling, birds are singing,
Odors sweet the wind is bringing;
Little girls and boys are straying,
Or in sunny places playing,
Seeking buttercups and clover,
While their hearts with joy run over.
But — what goose can't see it plainly? —
Spring for *us* is given mainly.
   Quack, quack! — quack, quack, quack!
Good soft mud and running water
   Now we shall not lack, — not lack!

GRANDPA'S CHERRY-TREE.

In grandpa's cherry-tree down by the barn
    What do you think I see?
Three little bright-eyed birdies,
    Having a regular spree.
A scarecrow, dressed in an old black coat,
    Hangs from the topmost limb;
But birds like these are not the birds
    To be afraid of him.

Arthur sits on a rocking bough,
    Eating all he can cram;
Dropping a cherry now and then
    In the hat of his brother Sam.

Robin's mouth and pockets are full;
　　So is his big straw hat;
And his apron makes him a " red breast : "
　　I'm very sure of that.

Bess, the mare, at the old barn-door
　　Stands quietly eating hay:
" What are those wild young colts about?."
　　I think I hear her say.
Now, whether she told mamma her thoughts,
　　Or grandpa suddenly feared
The boys were in mischief, I do not know ;
　　But they've all disappeared.

Ah! here they come with a joyful shout,
　　Straight up to the nursery-door ;
And with cherry skins and stems and juice
　　They are covered o'er and o'er.
Mother says, as she shakes her head,
　　" Boys will be boys," I see ;
But I fear some stomachs will ache to-night,
　　To pay for this little spree.

JACK'S MENAGERIE.

" THIS is our grand menagerie,
  Beneath the crooked cherry-tree.
  The exhibition now begins :
  Admittance, only thirteen pins ;
  And if the pins you cannot borrow,
  Why, then, we'll trust you till to-morrow.
  Don't be afraid to walk inside :
  The animals are safely tied.

" This is the elephant on the right :
  Don't meddle with him, or he'll bite.
  (He's Rover, Neddie's dog, you know.
  I wish he wouldn't fidget so !
  He doesn't think it fun to play
  Wild beast, and be chained up all day.)
  We'll feed him, pretty soon, with meat ;
  Though grass is what he ought to eat.

" In that box are the kangaroos :
  Go near and pat them if you choose ;
  (They're very much like Susie's rabbits,
  With just a change of name and habits.)
  You'll find them lively as a top :
  See, when I poke them, how they hop.
  They are not fierce ; but, oh ! take care :
  We now approach the grizzly bear.

" See her long claws, and only hear
  Her awful growl when I go near !
  We found her lying on a rug,
  And just escaped her fearful hug.
  It took some time to get her caged :
  She's terrible when she's enraged.
  (You think, perhaps, it's Mabel's cat,
  But don't you be too sure of that !)

" Here is the ostrich in her pen
  (It's Ernest's little bantam-hen) :
  She came from Africa, of course,
  And runs as fast as any horse ;
  And up above there is a bird
  Of whom you all have often heard, —
  The eagle (' That is not,' says Mary,
  ' A pretty name for my canary ')."

Just at this point, I grieve to say,
The elephant broke quite away,
O'erthrew the grizzly bear in rage,
Upset the eagle in his cage,
Flew at the kangaroos, and then
Attacked the ostrich in her pen.
Thus ended Jack's menagerie
Beneath the crooked cherry-tree !

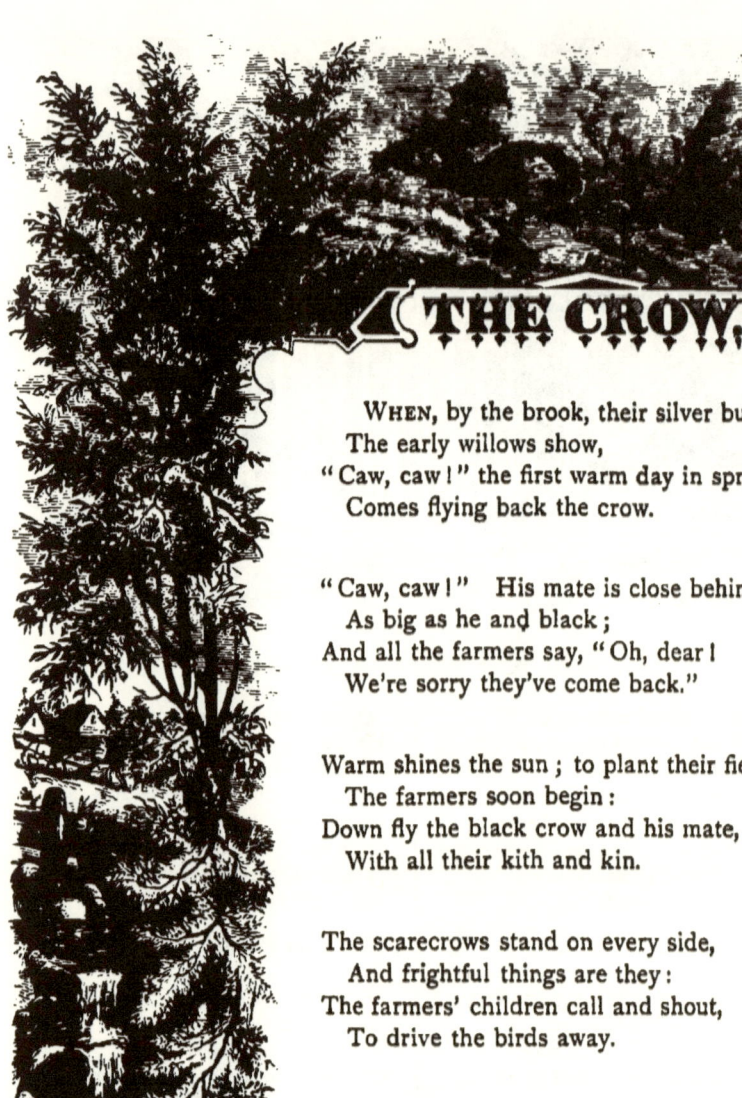

THE CROW.

WHEN, by the brook, their silver buds
  The early willows show,
"Caw, caw!" the first warm day in spring,
  Comes flying back the crow.

"Caw, caw!"   His mate is close behind,
  As big as he and black;
And all the farmers say, "Oh, dear!
  We're sorry they've come back."

Warm shines the sun; to plant their fields
  The farmers soon begin:
Down fly the black crow and his mate,
  With all their kith and kin.

The scarecrows stand on every side,
  And frightful things are they:
The farmers' children call and shout,
  To drive the birds away.

"Caw, caw, caw, caw!" what care the crows?
  The sprouting corn is sweet.
"Caw, caw!" they say; "we'll have a feast:
  Here's something good to eat."

The summer days are long and bright;
　The rain-drops softly fall:
The corn the crows have left behind
　Grows green and straight and tall.

But when the first ripe ears begin
　Among the husks to show,
"Caw, caw!" the whole flock after him,
　Comes flying back the crow.

"Caw, caw!" "Hark, hark!" the farmers say;
　"The crows begin to call:
Unless our corn we harvest now
　They'll surely eat it all."

They cut the corn-stalks down in haste;
　They store the ears away:
"Caw, caw!" the crow calls to his mate;
　"We will no longer stay."

They slowly spread their great black wings;
　They sail off, flying low;
And all the farmers say, "Good luck!
　"We're glad to see them go."

An easy life the crow may lead;
　But who would like to be
A visitor that one and all
　Are sorry when they see?

ON THE SEA-BEACH.

SEE the wild waves, how they toss up the spray!
Why should not we be as merry as they?
Come, my own sister, and walk on the sand,
Beside the blue ocean: oh! is it not grand?

Hark to the roar of the surf on the rocks!
The foam rushes onward like snowy-white flocks.
Then back the waves hurry away from the shore;
Then forward they rush with another wild roar.

The land, oh the land, my dear sister, for me!—
The good land, that stirs not for wind or for sea.
The ocean I love: but I love it the best
When I stand on the shore; for the shore is at rest.

THE FIRST POCKET.

WHAT is this tremendous noise?
What can be the matter?
Willie's coming up the stairs
With unusual clatter.
Now he bursts into the room,
Noisy as a rocket:
"Auntie! I am five years old —
And I've got a pocket!"

Eyes as round and bright as stars;
Cheeks like apples glowing;
Heart that this new treasure fills
Quite to overflowing.

" Jack may have his squeaking boots;
Kate may have her locket:
I've got something better yet, —
I have got a pocket! "

All too fresh the joy to make
Emptiness a sorrow:
Little hand is plump enough
To fill it — till to-morrow.
And, e'er many days were o'er,
Strangest things did stock it:
Nothing ever came amiss
To this wondrous pocket.

Leather, marbles, bits of string,
Licorice-sticks and candy,
Stones, a ball, his pennies too:
It was always handy.
And, when Willie's snug in bed,
Should you chance to knock it,
Sundry treasures rattle out
From this crowded pocket.

Sometimes Johnny's borrowed knife
Found a place within it:
He forgot that he had said,
" I want it *just a minute.*"
Once the closet-key was lost;
No one could unlock it:
Where do you suppose it was? —
Down in Willie's pocket!

WINTER.

WINTER day! frosty day!
God a cloak on all doth lay.
On the earth the snow he sheddeth;
O'er the lamb a fleece he spreadeth;
Gives the bird a coat of feather
To protect it from the weather;
Gives the children home and food.
Let us praise him! God is good.
Should the wind rise high and higher,
We can warm us by the fire:
Should the snow hide all the ground,
Warmth and shelter can be found.
Fuel waits us in the wood:
God is bountiful and good.

LITTLE BIRDIES.

WHAT do birdies dream of ?
Flowers and leaves and waving wheat,
Brooks and buds and mosses sweet,
Nooks all hidden from the heat,
　　Little birdies dream of.

What do birdies sing of ?
Morning dew-drops pearly fair,
Sunshine rippling down the air,
Heaven's rich beauty everywhere,
　　Little birdies sing of.

What are birdies proud of ?
Soft-lined houses upon the tree,
Baby birdies, one, two, three, —
These, my pet, you still may see
　　Little birdies proud of !

The Travelling Monkey.

My master grinds an organ:
   And I pick up his money;
And, when you see me doing it,
   You call it very funny.

But, though I dance and caper, still
   I feel at heart forlorn:
I wish I were in monkey-land, —
   The place where I was born!

There grow the great green cocoanuts
    Around the palm-tree's crown:
I used to climb and pick them off,
    And hear them — crack! — come down.

There, all day long, the purple figs
    Are dropping from the bough;
There hang the ripe bananas: oh,
    I wish I had some now!

I'd feast, and feast, and feast, and feast;
    And you should have a share.
How pleasant 'tis in monkey-land!
    Oh, would that I were there!

On some tall tree-top's highest bough,
    So high the clouds would sail
Just over me, I wish that I
    Were swinging by my tail!

I'd swing, and swing, and swing, and swing:
    How merry that would be!
But, oh! a travelling monkey's life
    Is very hard for me.

SONG OF THE BROOK

WHAT was the song of the meadow brook,
As under the willows his way he took?
    Wouldn't you like to know?
"Let me play a while as I will:
By and by I must turn the mill,
    As farther down I go.

"Daisies, hanging over my side,
Beautiful daisies, starry-eyed,
    Kiss me for I must go!
But think of me as I turn the wheel,
Grinding the corn into powdery meal
    And drifts of golden snow."

81

THE TEA-PARTY.

THE dolls had a tea-party : wasn't it fun !
In ribbons and laces they came, one by one.
We girls set the table, and poured out the tea ;
And each of us held up a doll on our knee.

You never saw children behave half so well :
Why, nobody had any gossip to tell !
And (can you believe it ?) for badness, that day,
No dolly was sent from the table away.

One dolly, however, the proudest one there,
Was driven almost to the verge of despair,
Because she had met with a simple mishap,
And upset the butter-plate into her lap.

The cups and the saucers they shone lily-white :
We helped all the dollies, they looked so polite.
We had cake and jam from our own pantry-shelves :
Of course, we did most of the eating ourselves.

But housewives don't know when their cares may begin.
The window was open, and pussy popped in :
He jumped on the table ; and what do you think ?
Down fell all the crockery there, in a wink.

We picked up the pieces, with many a sigh ;
Our party broke up, and we all said good-by :
Do come to our next one ; but then we'll invite
That very bad pussy to keep out of sight.

BERTHA TO BABY.

O LITTLE, little mother! I was once as small as you;
And I loved my dolly dearly, as you are loving too;
And they fed me with a spoon, because no teeth I had;
And a rattle or a sugar-plum would make me very glad.

But now I'm old and very wise, — yes, four years old am I:
My shoes and stockings I put on; I do not often cry;
And I can read "The Nursery;" and I can draw a house;
And with my pen and paper can be quiet as a mouse.

I have a little garden; it is planted full of flowers;
And there, each pleasant afternoon, I pass some happy hours;
And soon I hope, my little pet, that you'll be large enough
To go with me and play, when the weather is not rough.

WHO IS IT?

SURELY a step on the carpet I hear,
Some quiet mouse that is creeping so near.
Two little feet mount the rung of my chair:
True as I live, there is somebody there!
Ten lily fingers are over my eyes,
Trying to take me by sudden surprise;
Then a voice, calling in merriest glee,
"Who is it? Tell me, and you may go free."

"Who is it? Leave me a moment to guess.
Some one who loves me?" The voice answers, "Yes."
"Some one who's fairer to me than the flowers,
Brighter to me than the sunshiny hours?
Darling, whose white little hands make me blind
Unto all things that are dark and unkind;
Sunshine and blossoms, and diamond and pearl. —
Papa's own dear little, sweet little girl!"

MOON, SO ROUND AND YELLOW.

Moon, so round and yellow,
   Looking from on high,
How I love to see you
   Shining in the sky!
Oft and oft I wonder,
   When I see you there,
How they get to light you,
   Hanging in the air;

Where you go at morning,
   When the night is past,
And the sun comes peeping
   O'er the hills at last.
Some time I will watch you
   Slyly overhead,
When you think I'm sleeping
   Snugly in my bed.

GOOD-BY, BIRDS AND FLOWERS.

BUTTERCUP and daisy,
  Lily and bluebell,
Foxglove tall and violet,
  Rose and pimpernel;
Linnet, thrush, and blackbird,
  Finch, and Jenny Wren,
Good-by, pretty darlings!
  Soon we'll meet again.

Little stars will watch you
  Through the winter cold,
Till, with smiles of beauty,
  Springtime buds unfold:
Then I'll seek you early,
  Birds upon the tree!
Welcomes sweet you'll warble,
  Pretty ones, to me.

I will catch you, lily,
　Laughing in your bed;
I will kiss you, daisy,
　Till your cheeks be red.
You may hide, sweet pansy:
　I will find you out,
Where you, from your moss-couch,
　Shyly peep about.

Buttercup so dainty,
　I will have your gold ;
Bluebell, pink, and foxglove,
　All the gems you hold !
Good-by, then, till springtime,
　Till the rosy hours ;
Then will I be with you,
　Pretty birds and flowers !

PLAYING ROBINSON CRUSOE.

PLAY this is my little island
   In the middle of the floor;
And this arm-chair is my castle,
   With the ladder up before.

Play the cat is my man Friday;
   And the broom shall be my gun;
I've some wooden goats and a parrot:
   Please to call me Robinson.

Play I'm sighing for a vessel,
   And I'm on the watch for her;
Then the table is my big boat,
   Which I've tried in vain to stir.

Play the savages are coming:
    They are making for the land!
Now, I'm going to fire among them
    When they gather on the sand.

Oh! it's jolly on this island
    For an hour or so to stay;
But to live so far from mother!—
    I am glad it's only play!

THE SONG OF THE KETTLE.

My house is old, the rooms are low,
    The windows high and small;
And a great fireplace, deep and wide,
    Is built into the wall.

There, on a hanging chimney-hook,
  My little kettle swings;
And, in the dreary winter-time,
  How cheerily it sings!

My kettle will not sing to-day —
  What could it sing about ?
For it is empty, it is cold :
  The fire is all gone out.

Go, bring to me, to fill it up,
  Fresh water from the spring ;
And I will build a rousing fire,
  And that will make it sing!

Bring white bark from the silver birch,
  And pitch-knots from the pine ;
And here are shavings, long and white,
  That look as ribbons fine.

The little match burns faint and blue,
  But serves the fire to light;
And all around my kettle, soon,
  The flames are rising bright.

Crack, crack! begins the hemlock-branch,
  Snap, snap! the chestnut stick ;
And up the wide old chimney now
  The sparks are flying thick.

Like fire-flies on a summer night,
  They go on shining wings;
And, hark! above the roaring blaze
  My little kettle sings!

The robin carols in the spring;
In summer hums the bee:
But, in the dreary winter, give
The kettle's song to me.

———•o◦✕◦o•———

UNDER PAPA'S HELMET.

BY

ALFRED SELWYN.

———

DRAWING BY OSCAR PLETSCH.

———

OW, hurrah!
See him stand;
Helm on head,
Spear in hand!

Blow the horn,
Beat the drum,
Let the foe
Forward come!

Boy, may we
See the day

When all wars
Turn to play!

Swords and guns
Then shall be
Only toys
For you and me.

WHAT THE CAT SAID TO THE MONKEY.

You cowardly monkey, come out if you dare !
I'll teach you my dear little kittens to scare.
Because I had gone a few moments away,
You thought that to plague them was good monkey play.

But when I came back, just in season, I saw
What was up, and I gave you a pat with my paw :
It didn't set well, might I judge from your face.
What ails your poor arm ? and why that grimace ?

Now, here hangs my paw; and, if you're inclined
To try it again, 'twill be ready, you'll find.
And mark, Mr. Monkey, if up to your fun,
I'll show, to your sorrow, I have more than one.

So Velvetpaw, Whitefoot, and Darkey, don't fear !
No monkey shall harm you while mother is near.
The rascal who plagued you has found I am rough :
Of my paw and my claw he has had quite enough.

THE BIRD AND THE STAG.

LITTLE bird
  On the bough,
Tell me what
  You dream of now.

Gentle stag
  Beneath the tree,
Do not start
  At sight of me.

Live and gambol
  In this wood:
I'd not harm you
  If I could.

Sing, dear bird,
  And try to tell
Of the mate
  You love so well.

Pretty stag,
  Lie still, and hear
Birdie's song
  So sweet and clear.

Men with guns,
  Keep away!
Come not here
  To shoot and slay!

It would be
  A sin, I know,
So much joy
  To turn to woe.

WHAT DOES THE COCK SAY?

WHAT does the cock say every morn,
  Crowing so loud and shrill ?
You may hear the sound of his lusty horn
  Far over the distant hill.

" Get up, get up, get up!" he cries ;
  " Awake, awake, awake !
The sun is gilding the eastern skies ;
  And the day begins to break.

" Get up, and the daisies will kiss thy feet,
  The lark sing over thy head :
Far better be out with the flowers so sweet
  Than wasting the hours in bed !"

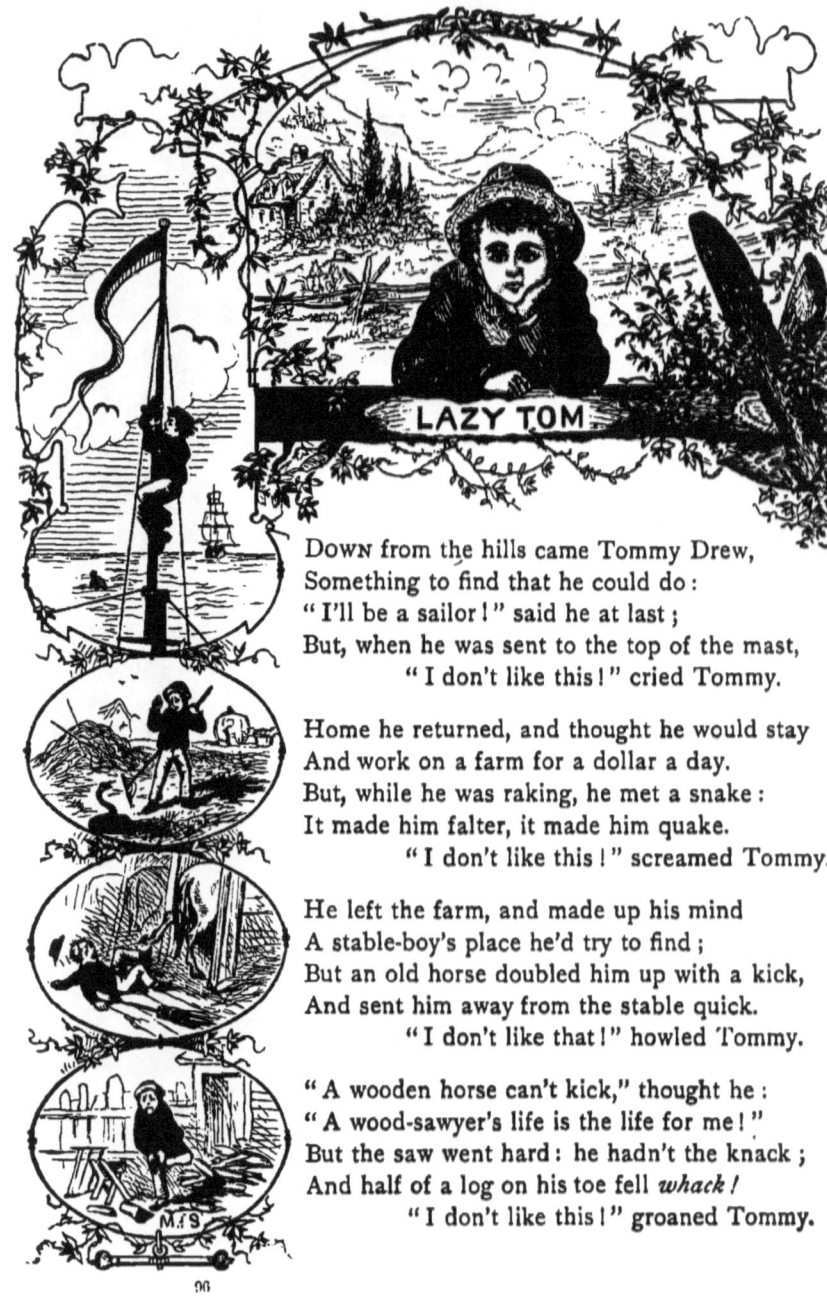

LAZY TOM

Down from the hills came Tommy Drew,
Something to find that he could do:
"I'll be a sailor!" said he at last;
But, when he was sent to the top of the mast,
        "I don't like this!" cried Tommy.

Home he returned, and thought he would stay
And work on a farm for a dollar a day.
But, while he was raking, he met a snake:
It made him falter, it made him quake.
        "I don't like this!" screamed Tommy.

He left the farm, and made up his mind
A stable-boy's place he'd try to find;
But an old horse doubled him up with a kick,
And sent him away from the stable quick.
        "I don't like that!" howled Tommy.

"A wooden horse can't kick," thought he:
"A wood-sawyer's life is the life for me!"
But the saw went hard: he hadn't the knack;
And half of a log on his toe fell *whack!*
        "I don't like this!" groaned Tommy.

LAZY TOM.

"A butcher I'll be, and cut up meat:
A good trade that; for people must eat;"
But, when with his cleaver he aimed a blow,
He hit the joint of his finger. "Oh!
    . I don't like that!" yelled Tommy.

"I'll get an organ, a monkey too,
And make my fortune," said Tommy Drew.
But he got a scratch on his lip one day;
And, though the monkey was only in play,
    "I don't like this!" whined Tommy.

"I'll get a gun: a sportsman I'll be!"
He spied a bird on the bough of a tree:
He lifted his gun, the trigger he drew;
It knocked him flat, and off the bird flew.
    "I don't like that!" shrieked Tommy.

"A fisherman's life just meets my wish:
I'll go to the rocks by the sea, and fish."
He threw his line; but a breeze from the south,
That blew the hook, made it catch in his mouth.
    "I don't like this!" moaned Tommy.

He came to a place where the sun shone clear;
And down he lay on a haycock near;
And up he looked at the sky so blue,
With nothing to sigh for, and nothing to do.
    "Ah! this I like," yawned Tommy.

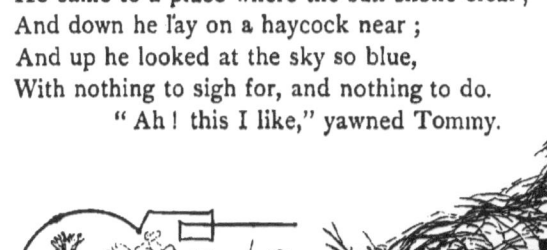

LEARNING TO FLY.

"Jump! you little birdie."
 Hark! the mother sings,
"Fly! you little birdie,
 Spread your little wings!"

See! the little birdie
 Jumps from off the bough:
Cunning little birdie,
 Do be careful now.

You're so very little,
 And the tree's so tall,
Oh! I tremble, birdie,
 Lest you get a fall.

Look! he's flying safely:
 He thinks not of fear;
For the little birdie
 Knows his mother's near.

THE FIRST LESSON.

Happy Mother Robin,
　Hard at work are you,
Teaching all your little ones
　What they ought to do.
Well they learn their lessons
　High up in the tree ;
Lowest class in singing :
　" Chee, chee, chee ! "

Baby's loving mother,
　Like Dame Robin there,
Has a little scholar
　Sunny, sweet, and fair ;

And she looks so earnest
　While she tries to say
This, her earliest lesson :
　" Day, day, day ! "

Baby and the birdies
　Soon drop off to rest ;
Then their mothers fold them
　In the cradle-nest.
Baby wins the medal,
　As you may suppose :
Only wait a little while
　And see how much it knows.

A SONG OF NOSES.

UNCAN has a nose,
　Points my finger at it :

Has a nose the hare,
　He will let you pat it.

Peacock has a nose,
　Very proud he's feeling.

Has a nose the bull,
　Soon he will be lowing.

Has a nose the fox,
　He is very knowing.

Has a nose the hog,
　Soon will he be squealing.

Tell me which of all these noses
Duncan now the best supposes.

MOTHER'S JOY AND MOTHER'S PLAGUE.

SAY, what shall I do with this baby ?
　In his crib now he ought to be sleeping ;
Yet here he is, wild for a frolic,
　And here wide awake he'll be keeping.

He wants all the folks to amuse him ;
　He thinks they can do nothing wiser :
But, baby, have mercy, I beg you !
　Go to sleep ; for you're not a late riser.

"Sleep, sleep, my dear, hush-a-by baby !"
　No, no !　See him laugh at the notion !
'Tis plain there's no peace for his mother ;
　For baby wants all her devotion.

GRANDPAPA'S SPECTACLES.

Grandpapa's spectacles cannot be found;
He has searched all the room, high and low, round and round :
Now he calls to the young ones, and what does he say ?
" Ten cents for the child who will find them to-day."

Then Henry and Nelly and Edward all ran ;
And a most thorough hunt for the glasses began ;
And dear little Nell, in her generous way,
Said, " *I'll* look for them, grandpa, without any pay ! "

All through the big Bible she searches with care,
That lies on the table by grandpapa's chair ;
They feel in his pockets ; they peep in his hat ;
They pull out the sofa ; they shake out the mat.

Then down on all-fours, like two good-natured bears,
Go Harry and Ned under tables and chairs,
Till, quite out of breath, Ned is heard to declare,
He believes that those glasses are *not anywhere.*

But Nelly, who, leaning on grandpapa's knee,
Was thinking most earnestly where they *could* be,
Looked suddenly up in the kind, faded eyes,
And her own shining brown ones grew big with surprise.

She clapped both her hands ; all her dimples came out :
She turned to the boys with a bright roguish shout, —
" You may leave off your looking, both Harry and Ned,
For there are the glasses on grandpapa's head ! "

OLD TRIM.

HERE's brave old Trim : I once with him
   Was walking near the docks ;
We heard a cry, both Trim and I, —
   The cry that always shocks.

" Help! boat, ahoy! See, there's a boy:
    Make haste, he's going down."
" There! watch him, Trim! in after him!
    We must not let him drown."

Through foam and splash Trim's quick eyes flash:
    He strikes out to the place;
And round and round, with eager bound,
    _ He watches for a trace.

A little hand comes paddling up,
    A face so wild and wan:
" Ah, Trim, he's there! Make haste, take care;
    And save him if you can!"

Oh! brave and bold, he seizes hold;
    His teeth are firmly set:
Now bear him near; there is no fear:
    The boy is breathing yet.

" Bravo, good Trim!" They welcome him,
    And clasp him round for joy;
Then homeward bear, with tender care,
    The pale, half-conscious boy.

O faithful Trim! "Would I sell him?"
    Inquired a curious elf:
" What, sell," I cried, "a friend so tried!
    I'd rather sell myself."

THE BIRDS AND THE POND-LILY.

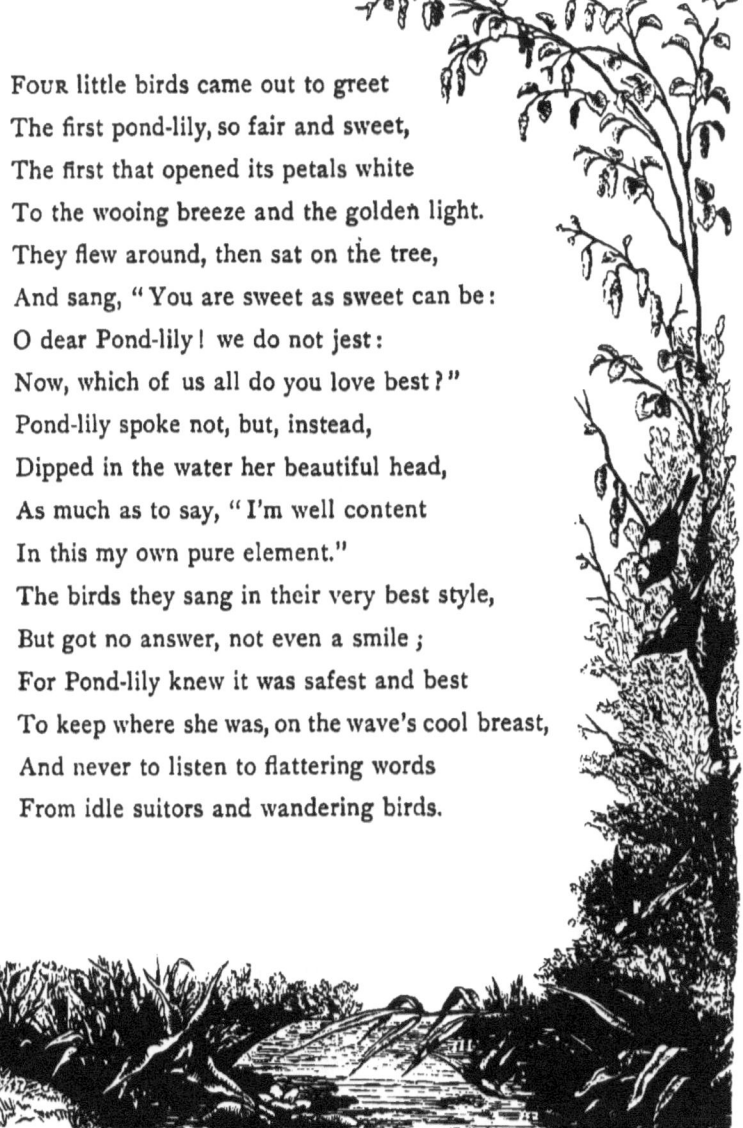

Four little birds came out to greet
The first pond-lily, so fair and sweet,
The first that opened its petals white
To the wooing breeze and the golden light.
They flew around, then sat on the tree,
And sang, "You are sweet as sweet can be:
O dear Pond-lily! we do not jest:
Now, which of us all do you love best?"
Pond-lily spoke not, but, instead,
Dipped in the water her beautiful head,
As much as to say, "I'm well content
In this my own pure element."
The birds they sang in their very best style,
But got no answer, not even a smile;
For Pond-lily knew it was safest and best
To keep where she was, on the wave's cool breast,
And never to listen to flattering words
From idle suitors and wandering birds.

THE BIRDS.

WHAT is it I hear,
　Very sweet, very clear?
Will it startle and wake
　The little Gold Head,
　Asleep in her bed?
　The darkness is gone,
　And the brightness of dawn
Is beginning to break.

　She hears; and her eyes
　Open wide in surprise,
While the birds sing, and sing,
　Singing far, singing near,
　Very sweet, very clear;
　And little Gold Head,
　Awake in her bed,
Cries out, "It is spring!"

CHIMNEY–TOPS.

" Ah ! the morning is gray ;
And what kind of a day
Is it likely to be ? "
" You must look up, and see
   What the chimney-tops say.

" If the smoke from the mouth
Of the chimney goes south.
'Tis the north wind, that blows
From the country of snows :
Look out for rough weather ;
The cold and the north wind
   Are always together.

" If the smoke pouring forth
From the chimney goes north,

A mild day it will be,
A warm time we shall see:
The south wind is blowing
From lands where the orange
  And fig trees are growing.

"But, if west goes the smoke,
Get your water-proof cloak
And umbrella about:
'Tis the east wind that's out.
A wet day you will find it:
The east wind has always
  A storm close behind it.

"But, if east the smoke flies,
We may look for blue skies:
Soon the clouds will take flight,
'Twill be sunny and bright.
The sweetest and best wind
Is surely that fair-weather
  Bringer, the west wind."

THE APPLE-TREE IN BLOOM.

OH, joy! 'tis the season of blossoms, —
The beautiful season of blossoms.
Has snow in the sunshine been falling?
Oh, no! 'tis the apple-tree blooming.

Pure white is each delicate blossom, —
Pure white, with a shading of crimson.
Oh! beautiful season of blossoms,
That gives us the apple-tree blooming.

Oh! come to the garden and see it, —
The apple-tree, old in its glory:
It sheds a whole carpet of blossoms,
And still seems as blooming as ever.

I love it, this season of blossoms, —
This beautiful season of blossoms.
Of all the fine sights you can show me,
Oh, show me the apple-tree blooming!

109

THE LILY-OF-THE-VALLEY.

"O LILY-OF-THE-VALLEY ! why will you be so coy,
  And hide away where few of us your beauty can enjoy ?
  Your little flowers, so white and pure, are fragrant to the smell ;
  Yet in the valley's cooling shade you always love to dwell."

"If you will listen very close, I'll tell you, little maid,
  Why thus I pass my lily life here in the cooling shade :
  If I were on the sunny bank, where all could see and praise,
  In such a glare I'd find it hard to live out half my days."

110

WAITING FOR THE MAY.

FROM out his hive there came a bee:
"Has spring-time come, or not?" said he.
Alone within a garden-bed
A small, pale snowdrop raised its head.
"'Tis March, this tells me," said the bee:
"The hive is still the place for me.
The day is chill, although 'tis sunny,
And icy cold this snowdrop's honey."

Again came humming forth the bee:
"What month is with us now?" said he.
Gay crocus-blossoms, blue and white
And yellow, opened to the light.
"It must be April," said the bee.
"And April's scarce the month for me.
I'll taste these flowers (the day is sunny),
But wait before I gather honey."

Once more came out the waiting bee.
" 'Tis come : I smell the spring ! " said he.
The violets were all in bloom ;
The lilac tossed a purple plume ;
The daff'dill wore a yellow crown ;
The cherry-tree a snow-white gown ;
And by the brook-side, wet with dew,
The early wild wake-robins grew.
" It is the May-time ! " said the bee,
" The queen of all the months for me !
The flowers are here, the sky is sunny :
'Tis now my time to gather honey ! "

WHILE OVER A WORM THESE LITTLE BIRDS FIGHT,
TO SEIZE THEM THE HAWK SWOOPS DOWN FROM HER FLIGHT.
AND SO, MY DEAR CHILDREN, BEWARE OF A QUARREL :
A HAWK MAY BE WATCHING YOU — THAT IS MY MORAL.

SANTA CLAUS.

Santa Claus came here last night
    On his flight.
Down the chimney-top he flew :
He had lots of work to do,
    Well he knew.

So he heaped the stockings high,
    Said " Good-by."
Now, of toys he had no lack :
They were carried on his back,
    In a sack.

What did little Flora find ? —
    Flora kind.
Why, a doll with golden hair,
Candies, and a tiny chair,
    I declare !

What did bright-eyed Georgie get ? —
Mamma's pet.
Can't you guess ?   A tiny gun ;
But you see it's only one
Made for fun.

Here's what lazy Joseph found,
Looking round.
It was shocking !
In his stocking,
There was nothing, you must know,
But a big hole at the toe,
Lazy Joe !

EVERY day when school is done,
We play at ball : it's splendid fun.

ONE year old to-day!
  See our baby bright!
Ring the bells! Be gay!
  What a pretty sight!

Beat the drums, and blow
  All the trumpets too!
Let the people know
  What they now must do.

They must come and greet
  Baby as he lies
Looking out, so sweet,
  With his thoughtful eyes.

Tell us, little man,
  What your heart is saying;
Tell us, if you can,
  Where your thoughts are
    straying.

A SUMMER DAY.

THIS is the way the morning dawns:
    Rosy tints on flowers and trees,
    Winds that wake the birds and bees,
    Dewdrops on the fields and lawns, —
This is the way the morning dawns.

This is the way the sun comes up:
    Gold on brooks and glossy leaves,
    Mist that melts above the sheaves,
    Vine and rose and buttercup, —
This is the way the sun comes up.

This is the way the rain comes down :
Tinkle, tinkle, drop by drop,
Over roof and chimney-top ;
Boughs that bend, and skies that frown, —
This is the way the rain comes down.

This is the way the river flows :
Here a whirl, and there a dance,
Slowly now, then like a lance,
Swiftly to the sea it goes, —
This is the way the river flows.

This is the way the birdie sings :
"Baby-birdies in the nest,
You I surely love the best ;
Over you I fold my wings," —
This is the way the birdie sings.

This is the way the daylight dies :
Cows are lowing in the lane,
Fire-flies wink on hill and plain ;
Yellow, red, and purple skies, —
This is the way the daylight dies.

A LITTLE GIRL'S GOOD-BY.

GOOD-BY, daisy, pink, and rose,
  And snow-white lily too;
Every pretty flower that grows:
  Here's a kiss for you.

Good-by, merry bird and bee;
  And take this tiny song
For the ones you sang to me
  All the summer long.

Good-by, mossy little rill,
  That shivers in the cold:
Leaves that fall on vale and hill
  Cover you with gold.

A sweet good-by to birds that roam,
  And rills and flowers and bees;
But, when winter's gone, come home
  As early as you please.

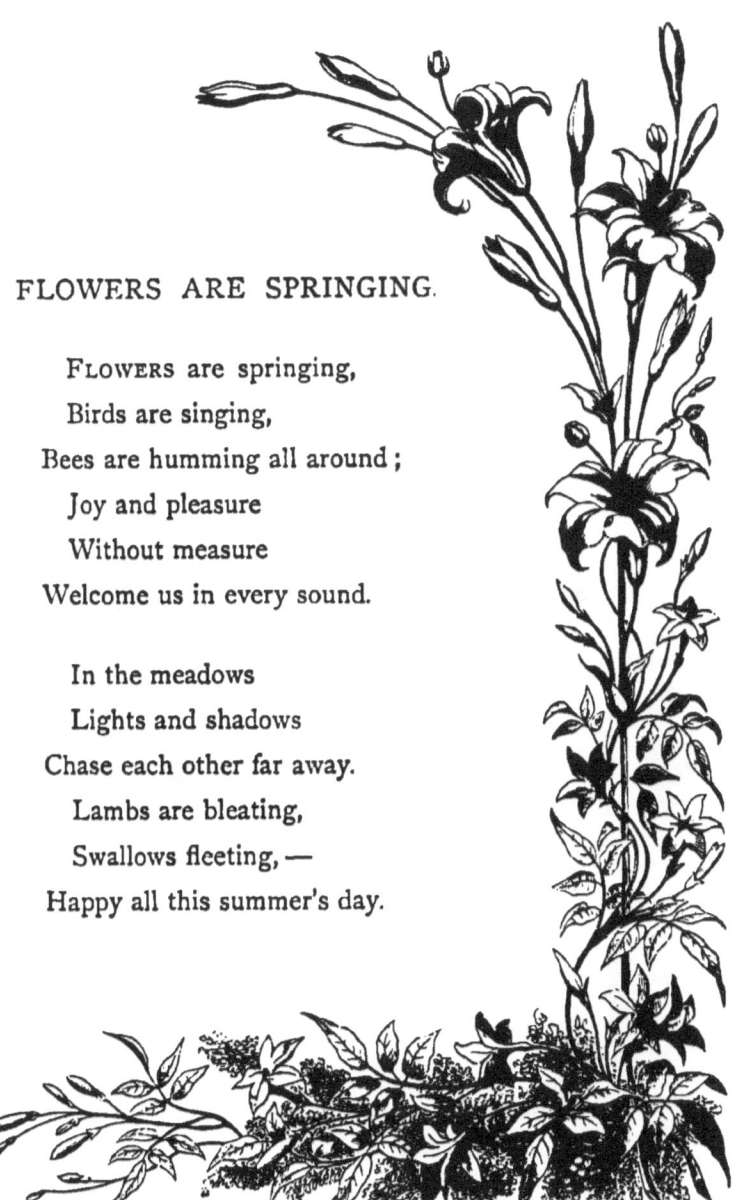

FLOWERS ARE SPRINGING.

FLOWERS are springing,
  Birds are singing,
Bees are humming all around ;
  Joy and pleasure
  Without measure
Welcome us in every sound.

  In the meadows
  Lights and shadows
Chase each other far away.
  Lambs are bleating,
  Swallows fleeting, —
Happy all this summer's day.

THE SKIPPING-ROPE.

See Nora with her skipping-rope:
    How fast she makes it fly!
She will not jump too much, I hope,
    But soon will put it by.

Good things are good while rightly used;
    But they will end in harm
If in the use they are abused,
    And then they lose their charm.

CLEVER JACK.

I.

JACKY by the river-side,
  Jacky by the river :
He let his clothes go all in holes,
  And so he had to shiver.

II.

Jacky by the river-side
  Often used to linger :
He caught a fish, but let it go
  Because it bit his finger.

III.

Jack by the river-side
  Got into a boat,
And threw a millstone in the tide,
  To see if it would float.

IV.

Jack by the river-side
  Found a maiden fair :
He was stupid, she was stupid ;
  So they were a pair.

V.

Jack by the river-side,—
"Maiden fair," said he,
"You're a noodle, I'm a noodle:
Will you marry me?"

VI.

"Jack by the river-side,"—
Thus the maiden said,—
"You've no money, I've no money:
How shall we be fed?"

VII.

Says Jack by the river-side,
"That needn't cause us sorrow:
Suppose we go without to-day,
And hope for bread to-morrow."

VIII.

Says Jack by the river-side,
"See, this will help us through:
We'll go and visit all our friends,
As many others do."

IX.

So Jack by the river-side
Went bowing round about;
And one friend would not let him in,
And the other turned him out.

X.

Jack by the river-side
Said, "'Twon't do to fail:
We'll take a basket for a house,
An egg-chest, or a pail."

XI.

Says Jack by the river-side,
"A basket sure is best;
And we'll sit as snugly there
As birds within their nest."

XII.

Jack by the river-side
In his house you may behold;
But, in the winter, wife and he
Both found it rather cold.

XIII.

Jack by the river-side
Now thought of singing small;
But fortune smiled at last on him,
And made amends for all.

XIV.

One day, when wife went out to spin,
And he went out to plough,
They found an empty washing-tub;
And there they're living now.

APRIL   FOOL.

WHAT are the children all about?
  Mischief is certainly brewing :
When four little heads are in a bunch,
  I know there'll be something doing.

Hark ! what a merry, noisy shout,
  As away they suddenly scatter !
Papa has sweetened his tea with salt,
  And doesn't know what's the matter.

Mother, who says, " You can't catch me ! "
  Her breakfast just ready to swallow,
Finds that the egg she likes so well
  (How strange !) is perfectly hollow.

Bridget, with dish-cloth pinned behind
  By fingers that stealthily handle,
Is patiently trying, with all her might,
  To light — a potato-candle !

But, ah, you rogues ! though you had your fun,
  The fun was not all for you ;
And you found, before the day was done,
  We could have our nonsense too.

For Dick, who thinks maple-sugar nice,
  Took a bite of soap so yellow !
Tom tasted a doughnut of cotton-wool,
  And got laughed at well, poor fellow !

And when mother sent to the thread-store near,
  The little ones, Kate and Willie,
For a skein of sky-blue scarlet silk,
  They came back looking quite silly.

Our jokes were only innocent fun ;
  And now let me give you a rule :
Don't ever be vulgar or rude or unkind
  In playing at April Fool.

THE TRADESPEOPLE.

THE swallow is a mason ;
  And underneath the eaves
He builds a nest, and plasters it
  With mud and hay and leaves.

The woodpecker is hard at work :
  A carpenter is he ;
And you may find him hammering
  His house high up a tree.

The bullfinch knows and practises
  The basketmaker's trade :
See what a cradle for his young
  The little thing has made !

Of all the weavers that I know,
  The chaffinch is the best :
High on the apple-tree he weaves
  A cosey little nest.

The goldfinch is a fuller :
  A skilful workman he !
Of wool and threads he makes a nest
  That you would like to see.

The cuckoo laughs to see them work :
  " Not so," he says, " we do :
My wife and I take others' nests,
  And live at ease — cuckoo ! "

THE BIRD'S RETURN.

"Where have you been, little birdie, —
Where have you been so long?"

"Warbling in glee
Far o'er the sea,
And learning for you a new song,
My sweet, —
Learning for you a new song."

"Why did you go, little birdie, —
Why did you go from me?"

"Winter was here,
Leafless and drear;
And so I flew over the sea,
My sweet, —
So I flew over the sea."

"What did you see, little birdie, —
What did you see each day?"

"Sunshine and flowers,
Blossoms and bowers,
And pretty white lambkins at play,
My sweet, —
Pretty white lambkins at play."

"Who kept you safe, little birdie, —
Who kept you safe from harm?"

"The Father of all,
Of great and of small:
He sheltered me under his arm,
My sweet, —
Under his dear, loving arm."

AT THE PUMP.

PUMP away, pump away, sister of ours!
Water's the thing for us and the flowers;
Roses and children would droop, day by day,
Had they no water: so, Jane, pump away.

Water for washing, and water for drinking;
There's nothing like water, fresh water, I'm thinking:
Put nothing but water in cup and in pitcher,
And then, merry men, you'll be wiser and richer.

THE SWALLOWS.

SINCE one swallow does not make a summer,
Come, O West Wind! come with many a comer!
Let the swallows come with spring-days sunny:
They shall have a home; we'll ask no money.

See them gather! — hear them scold and chatter! —
On the fence: now, what can be the matter?
Little birds should loving be, and quiet:
Why, then, swallows, why, then, make a riot?

See them! hear them! they are welcome, very:
Now we soon shall have the spring-days merry.
Time of blossoms, time of song and flowers:
O the happy, happy spring-time hours!

www.ingramcontent.com/pod-product-compliance
Lightning Source LLC
Chambersburg PA
CBHW032009010726
47493CB00007B/2339